Clorinda
Takes Flight

Robert Kinerk

Illustrated by
Steven Kellogg

A PAULA WISEMAN BOOK
Simon & Schuster Books for Young Readers
New York London Toronto Sydney

Clorinda the cow took the sun now and then
in the back of a friend's house, the farmhand named Len.
When a swallow swooped by, though, she leaped up to follow.

She raced past the barn,

out the gate,

down a hollow.

"Oh, to fly! What delight! What a treat! What a thrill!"
she cried as she reached the tip-top of a hill.
"Good-bye, graceful swallow! How sweetly you soar!
I've never, not once, in my life soared before.
But I want to be free like you birds in that sky,
and I promise you now that I *will* learn to fly!"

Clorinda ran straight to her friend, the pig Hop.
She said, "I must fly!" But the pig told her, "Stop!
We all want to fly. It's a dream we all share.
But please, my good friend . . . a cow in the air?
You haven't got feathers, Clorinda, nor wings.
And to fly, I assure you, requires such things."

Clorinda's eyes brightened. She said, "Please explain
why a cow isn't able to fly her own plane?"

"What plane?" asked the pig.
He was clearly not thrilled.
But the cow very cheerfully said,
"One we'll build!"

She danced to her truck
with her face all aglow,
so happy the pig
couldn't bear to say no.
"I knew I could count on you, Hop,"
said the cow.

"And Lenny will help us.
I'm sure he'll know how
to cope with a problem,
if one should arise.
Like you, my good friend,
Lenny's kind and he's wise."

They drove to the DUMP

and found boxes and cases
that they thought they could use
for the struts and the braces.

The wheels that they needed they couldn't find cheap,
so they borrowed a pair off of Lenny's old jeep.

To cover the wings and the long fuselage,
they stripped the tin roof off of Lenny's garage.

The motor they got from Len's washing machine,
after first making sure all his laundry was clean.

And finally the friends, with some turns on a screw,
got the prop fastened on—and with that they were through.

Len, Hop, and the cow made a very good team.
The guys kept her working, and she helped them dream.

"Time for the test flight! Let's put on our goggles!"
Clorinda declared as Hop wiggled the toggles.
Len cranked the engine. It gave a loud cough.
They roared through the garden, and then . . . **they took off!**

"Hooray!" cried the cow as they flew through the skies.
Her copilot whimpered and covered his eyes.
For the wings had come loose. And so had the rudder.
The plane gave a wheeze, and it started to shudder.
Downward they plunged, but by some lucky stroke,
the plane came to rest at the top of an oak.

Poor Hop. He was gasping
and clutching his heart.
"Clorinda," he said,
"I believed from the start
your dream was delightful
but slightly unsound,
and that creatures like us
ought to stay on the ground."
Clorinda said sadly,
"I guess that is true.
Flight is a thing
that a cow cannot do."

"And yet," observed Len as he helped them descend, "your plane *did* take off. So I'd say, as your friend, your goal was achieved. You guys did it! You flew!"

"Well," murmured Hop, "I suppose that is true."

With the pig's help and Len's, she was well on her way
to planning the next flight, and then several more.
"What *helpers*!" she said. "This is what friends are for!"

They constructed a rocket. The rocket went *Phhhhfftt*.
But that didn't matter. The friends wouldn't quit.

"A copter!" they cried. They all worked nonstop.

It went up with a ROAR . . .

and
came
down
with
a
PLOP.

Then over the barn
rose a glorious moon.
It was round. It was full.
It was like a balloon.
"A balloon!" the cow shouted.
"That's perfect. Oh, wow!"
"Yes!" cried the pig.
"Let's get started right now!

There—on the wash line—
are clothes of all sorts.
We can make our balloon
out of socks, sheets, and shorts!"

"A balloon," observed Len, "as you may be aware,
in order to rise will need lots of hot air.
With glasses and mirrors the air could be heated."
They worked until dawn, when the job was completed.

The magnified light Len supplied did the trick.
The balloon filled with air, and Clorinda said, "Quick!
Into the basket!" She clambered aboard.
Hop squeezed in behind her, and . . . upward they soared!

"Where's Len?" they both said
as they rose in the sky.

Len was still on the ground. He was waving good-bye,
for in all their haste about what they would do,
they'd forgotten to wait until he climbed in too.

Through cloud banks and rainbows, past ravens and cranes,
they flew over mountains and rivers and plains.
Their hearts swelled with joy in the wide, immense sky.
"Oh, Hop." Clorinda sighed. "It's lovely to fly."

New York and the ocean both sped by, and then
they heard the rich chimes of the famous Big Ben.

The Big Ben of England! In the crowds down below,
people yelled, "Splendid!" and "Jolly good show!"
They heard drums, fifes, and trumpets, and bagpiping men.
Clorinda said sadly, "We should have brought Len.
This concert is something he'd love to attend.
It's great fun for us, but I do miss our friend."

As for Len, in his dreams he had never foreseen
that his friends would appear on the news with the queen!

The queen told them, "Bravo! Never before
have a cow and a pig ballooned to our shore.

"So kneel, noble heroes, while we, with our sword,
grant you both knighthood. Now name your reward."

The cow thought and thought, and the pig scratched his head.
They whispered a moment, then both of them said,
"Our helper was Len, and how happy he'd be
if we could bring back to him some of your tea."

"How kind," said the queen, "that you've thought of your friend.
As for me, I must say, I'm delighted to send,
through you, to this Lenny, the very same tea
he'd get if he came for a chit-chat with me."

With that they said thanks, for the lengthening shade
warned both of the friends that the day would soon fade.

Her majesty's staff helped them load and untie
and cheered as they watched the balloon climb the sky.

Heading west, ever west,
over seas laced with foam,
they caught sight at last
of their own farmland home.

There Len with a welcoming cheer lent a hand
and helped them touch down on the best place to land.

They gave Len a hug. Then the cow with a grin
presented the tea in its decorative tin.

And they promised their friend that the next time they flew,
they'd take him along so he'd meet the queen too.

And under the stars, in the moon's silver beams,
they talked of adventures, of friendship, and dreams.

To Anne, who keeps me flying
—R. K.

For Poppy, who flew around the world
With love
—S. K.

SIMON & SCHUSTER BOOKS FOR YOUNG READERS
An imprint of Simon & Schuster Children's Publishing Division
1230 Avenue of the Americas, New York, New York 10020
Text copyright © 2007 by Robert Kinerk
Illustrations copyright © 2007 by Steven Kellogg
All rights reserved, including the right of reproduction in whole or in part in any form.
SIMON & SCHUSTER BOOKS FOR YOUNG READERS is a trademark of Simon & Schuster, Inc.
Book design by Einav Aviram
The text for this book is set in Lomba.
The illustrations for this book are rendered in mixed water-based medium.
Manufactured in China
2 4 6 8 10 9 7 5 3 1
Library of Congress Cataloging-in-Publication Data
Kinerk, Robert.
Clorinda takes flight / Robert Kinerk ; illustrated by Steven Kellogg.— 1st ed.
p. cm.
"A Paula Wiseman Book."
Summary: Using determination and vision, Clorinda the cow and her friend Hop the pig build a variety
of flying machines, hoping to fulfill her desire to take flight.
ISBN-13: 978-0-689-86864-1
ISBN-10: 0-689-86864-2
[1. Flight—Fiction. 2. Perseverance (Ethics)—Fiction. 3. Airplanes—Fiction. 4. Friendship—Fiction.
5. Cows—Fiction. 6. Stories in rhyme.] I. Kellogg, Steven, ill. II. Title.
PZ8.3.K566 Cl 2005
[E]—dc22
2003019273